World's Best Mama

DISNEP'S

A Winnie the Pooh First Reader

World's Best Mama

by Isabel Gaines

ILLUSTRATED BY Mark Marderosian and Fred Marvin

DISNEP
PRESS

NEW YORK

Library of Congress Catalog Card Number: 99-68495

ISBN: 0-7868-4368-3

For more Disney Press fun, visit www.disneybooks.com

World's Best Mama

One sunny spring day,
Tigger and Roo were out
bouncing.

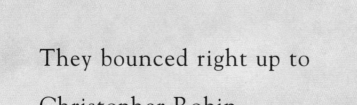

They bounced right up to

Christopher Robin.

"Hello, Christopher Robin!"
they said.

"Hello, Roo! Hello, Tigger!"
said Christopher Robin.

"Roo, I have been looking for you.

Do you know

what day tomorrow is?"

Roo thought for a moment.

"My birthday?" he asked.

"No, Roo!" said Christopher Robin.

"It's Mother's Day!"

"Oh goody," said Roo.

"I want to give something

extra special to Mama."

"Tiggers love surprises,"

said Tigger.

"Do mothers like them, too?"

"I think mine would," said Roo.

11

"We can have a surprise party,"

said Christopher Robin.

"And everyone can bring her

a present."

Christopher Robin, Roo, and Tigger

invited all of their friends

in the Hundred-Acre Wood.

They asked everyone

to bring a gift for Kanga.

The next morning,

Roo woke up with a start.

"Oh no!" he said.

"I forgot to get Mama

a present!"

Roo looked through his toys.

Maybe there was one Mama would like.

But they were all for young Roos,

not grown-up mamas.

15

Roo heard a knock at the front door.

He ran out of his room

just as Kanga opened it.

"HAPPY MOTHER'S DAY!"
everyone shouted.

"Surprise, Mama!" cried Roo.

17

Kanga smiled from ear to ear.

"Thank you, Roo!

Thank you, everyone!"

she said.

"Please come in."

"This is your day, Mama,"
said Roo. "You sit down
while we celebrate you—
the world's best mama."

Roo started the party.

"Mama, here is your first present.

It is from Eeyore!"

Eeyore gave Kanga a small bunch
of sagging flowers.

"Guess they need water," he said.

"Thank you, Eeyore," said Kanga.

"Next, Tigger has something special for you, Mama," said Roo.

Tigger bounced up carrying a huge
bunch of flowers.

"Happy Mother's Day!"
he said.
"Oh, Tigger!"
said Kanga.
"These are beautiful."

"My flowers don't look

so nice next to Tigger's,"

said Eeyore.

"Your flowers are very pretty,

too, Eeyore,"

said Kanga.

"Now," said Roo,

"Christopher Robin's, Rabbit's,

Piglet's, and Pooh's gifts!"

Christopher Robin carried over

a tray of muffins.

Behind him was Rabbit
with a basket of fresh vegetables
from his garden.

Then came Piglet
with a cake.
It was bigger than
he was!

Pooh followed Piglet
with a jar of honey.

"Next, Owl will say a poem,"
said Roo.
Owl stood in the
center of the room.

He cleared his throat and then began.

"Kanga is a mother
unlike any other.
She cares for one and all,
whenever we do fall."

29

Everyone clapped.

Kanga clapped the loudest.

Then there was silence.

What was next?

Roo started to cry.

"Roo, dear," said Kanga,

"what is the matter?"

"I forgot to get you a present,"

said Roo.

"You have already given me
the best Mother's Day present
ever," said Kanga.

"I did?" asked Roo.

"Yes!" answered Kanga.

"I am the luckiest mother

in the world

because I have YOU for a son."

33

Roo smiled a huge smile.

He gave his mom

one more present—

a great big Mother's Day hug!

Can you match the words with the pictures?

flowers

mother

toys

hug

Roo

Fill in the missing letters.

muffi_s

ca_e

_igger

ea_

ve_etables

Winnie the Pooh First Readers

Follow all the adventures
of Pooh and his friends!